Disney
PRINCESS
Beauty and the Beast

Retold by Amelia Hansen
Illustrated by Angel Rodríguez

Bath · New York · Cologne · Melbourne · Delhi
Hong Kong · Shenzhen · Singapore

Once upon a time, an old woman came to the castle of a spoiled and selfish prince. She offered him a single rose in exchange for shelter. But the prince turned her away.

The old woman was really an enchantress!

She cast a spell on the castle.

Unless the prince could learn to love – and earn

someone's love in return – before the last rose petal

fell, he would remain

a beast

forever.

In a sleepy little village not far away, there lived a beautiful girl named Belle. She dreamed of having adventures like those in her **favourite** books.

In the same village there lived a strong, powerful man named Gaston. Gaston wanted to marry Belle because she was so **beautiful.**

Gaston was handsome ...
but **very vain.**

Belle wanted
nothing
to do with him.

One day, Belle's father, Maurice,
set out for the fair with a new invention.
"Goodbye, Papa!" Belle called.

"Good luck!"

But soon Maurice became lost in the woods.
His horse, Phillipe, got scared and ran away.
And then
wolves attacked!

Maurice
escaped to a
nearby castle.

It was the **Beast's castle!** Maurice was amazed by the enchanted servants. Lumiere and Mrs Potts welcomed him, but Cogsworth was worried the Beast would find Maurice and be angry.

The Beast was furious to find a stranger in his home.

"So, you've come to stare at the Beast, have you?"

He locked Maurice in the

dungeon.

When Phillipe returned home alone, Belle
knew something **awful** had happened.
She rode off at once to find her father.

When Belle arrived, the Beast refused to let Maurice go.
She looked up at him bravely. "Take me, instead."

"You must promise to stay here forever," the Beast warned.

Belle was very scared. But she had to save her father.

"You have my word,"

she said.

While Mrs Potts and Chip tried to **cheer** Belle up ...

... the servants urged the Beast to be **gentle.**

That night, Belle discovered
the enchanted rose.

The Beast lashed out in **anger**
when Belle tried to touch the rose.
Frightened, Belle
fled from the castle.

The wolves chased Belle.
Desperately,
she tried to
scare them away.

Then the Beast appeared!
He fought off the wolves,
but they **hurt** him.

Belle wanted to leave, but
she knew the Beast needed her
help.

Back at the castle, Belle thanked the Beast for

saving her life.

"You're welcome," he replied.

They started to get along better after that.

One evening, the
Beast invited Belle to
a **special** dinner.

Belle was **excited.**

The Wardrobe helped her
choose the perfect outfit –
a **beautiful** golden
ball gown with matching
gloves and shoes.

The Beast was on his very best behaviour. When the music started, Belle pulled him into the ballroom to dance with her.

The Beast knew he had

fallen in love.

The Beast let Belle use his magic
mirror to see her father.

It showed Maurice
in **trouble!**

"Then you must go to him," the Beast told Belle.
He set his true love free, along with any hope of
breaking his curse.
He gave her the mirror so she would always
remember him.

At home, Maurice was overjoyed to see Belle. But soon there was a knock at the door.

The villagers thought Maurice was **crazy** because of his stories about the Beast. They had come to take him away!

"My father's not crazy!" Belle said. She showed them
the Beast in the mirror. Gaston convinced the others
that the Beast was

dangerous.

He led them towards the castle to kill the Beast!

Belle was devastated.

She had to warn her
friend!

Gaston was the first to arrive at the castle.

He attacked,

but the Beast didn't fight back.

With Belle no longer in his life, nothing seemed

to matter.

"No!" shouted Belle.

When the Beast heard Belle's voice, his strength

returned. He grabbed Gaston and whispered,

"Get out."

But Gaston stabbed the Beast from behind!
The Beast **roared** in pain and
Gaston, startled, fell to
the rocks below.

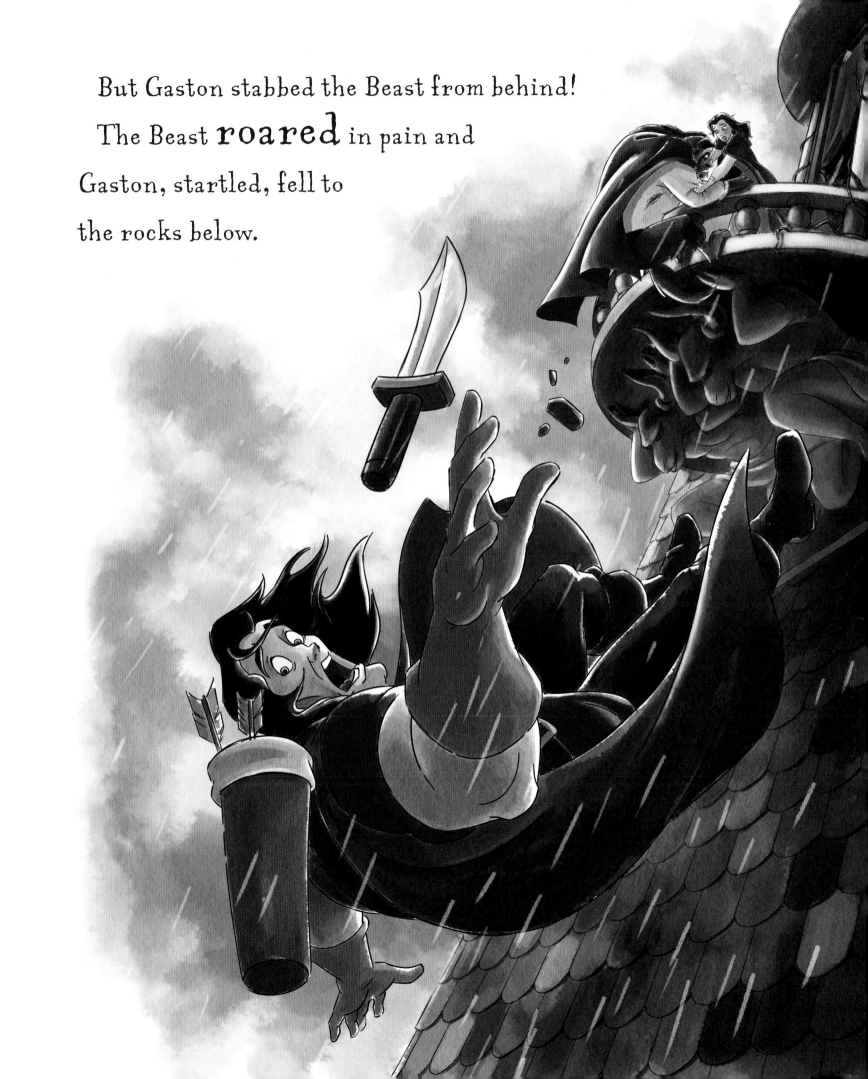

Belle pulled the Beast to safety, but he was badly hurt.

"Please don't leave me," Belle said, sobbing.

"I love you."

With those three words, the **spell** was broken!

Belle stared as the Beast
transformed

into a handsome man.

Happy cries rang out as the servants turned back into humans.
But no one was more **joyful** than Belle and her prince.